Our King Has Horns!

Retold by
Richard Pevear

Illustrated by
Robert Rayevsky

Macmillan Publishing Company
New York

Collier Macmillan Publishers
London

Macmillan Publishing Company, 866 Third Avenue, New York, NY 10022
Collier Macmillan Canada, Inc.
Printed and bound in Japan
First American Edition

10 9 8 7 6 5 4 3 2 1

The text of this book is set in 14 point Palatino.
The illustrations are rendered in ink and watercolor.
Library of Congress Cataloging-in-Publication Data
Pevear, Richard, date.
Our king has horns!
Summary: Having discovered the king's horns
while cutting his hair, a young barber is sworn
to secrecy or he will lose his life.
[1. Folklore. 2. Barbers—Folklore. 3. Kings,
queens, rulers, etc.—Folklore] I. Rayevsky,
Robert, ill. II. Title.
PZ8.1.P54Qu 1987 398.2'2 [E] 86-23525
ISBN 0-02-773920-1

To Larissa
R.P. and R.R.

Once there was a king who had horns on his head. No one knew why the king had horns. No one even knew he *had* them, because he never appeared without his crown.

The only people who learned of the king's horns were the barbers who cut the royal hair. The king had the barbers thrown into prison as soon as they had finished their work, and they were never heard from again.

One day a young barber moved to the royal city with his old mother, his young wife, and his little dog. He opened a shop and was soon busy cutting hair. Merchants, storekeepers, tradesmen and their apprentices crowded into his shop, gossiping and waiting for their turn in the chair. His mirror flashed, his scissors flew, and overnight the young barber prospered.

On a spring morning when his shop was crowded as usual and the young barber was busily snipping away, a royal messenger appeared at the door. He strode up to the young barber and said in a loud voice, "You are summoned to the palace by order of the king, for the purpose of administering the royal haircut."

The messenger pointed at two burly guards waiting outside. "These two gentlemen will accompany you," he said. Then he turned on his heel and strode out of the shop.

The young barber felt greatly honored. Imagine, he was to administer the royal haircut! He gazed proudly around the room. But his customers all looked pale and frightened.

"What's wrong?" he asked.

Finally an old merchant spoke. "It is undoubtedly a great honor to be summoned to the palace to cut the king's hair," he said, "but it is also a terrible misfortune."

"A misfortune? Why?" asked the barber.

"Because no one who has been so greatly honored has ever returned from the palace."

His customers filed out of the shop, leaving the young barber staring after them.

"Make it snappy!" growled one of the guards, poking his head into the doorway.

"Mustn't keep the king waiting," said the other.

The young barber told his family what had happened. They wept and said their last farewells. Then off he went between the two guards, preparing himself for the worst.

When he arrived at the palace, he was ushered into a small room with a door on each side and no windows. The door by which he had entered was locked behind him, and he stood alone in the room with his comb and scissors in his hand and his mirror under his arm.

Soon the opposite door opened and the king stepped into the room. The young barber bowed deeply, not daring to raise his eyes.

The king locked his own door, crossed the room to make sure that the other door was locked, then sat down in the one piece of furniture the room contained: a large, leather-cushioned barber's chair.

"Stop bowing and start working," said the king. And he removed his crown.

"It is my privilege to obey Your Majesty," said the young barber. He looked up, and there before him sat the king with a fine pair of horns on his head. They curled around like the horns of an old ram and ended in two sharp points.

That's the strangest thing I ever saw, the young barber thought. But he let nothing show on his face, and he did not say a word. He simply set about cutting the king's hair.

When he had finished his work, he held up his mirror for the king. The king looked at himself. Then he looked at the young barber, narrowed his eyes, and asked, "What do you think?"

"As skillful a haircut as I've ever given, Your Majesty," said the young barber.

"But what do you think?" the king insisted.

"The noblest head I've ever had the honor of working on," said the young barber. "A most royal head. Truly the head of a king!"

The king liked the way the young barber behaved. He took a last admiring look in the mirror and put on his crown.

"You may go," he said, unlocking the door. "But I warn you, if you tell a single soul what you have seen, it will cost you your head!"

The young barber bowed and left the palace.

When he reached home, everyone surrounded
him and began asking how he had saved himself.
But the young barber clamped his mouth shut and
would not say a word—not to his old mother, not to
his young wife, not even to his little dog.

Yet he wanted very much to tell *someone* that the king had horns! He was so full of his secret that he began to swell up. The longer he was silent, the rounder he grew, until his belly touched the tip of his chin.

His customers took the change in him as a sign of prosperity. His old mother accused his young wife of spoiling him, and his wife accused his mother of the same. Only the barber knew the real reason for the change.

Finally he could stand his secret no more. He was ready to burst. Early one morning he slipped out of town, went far away to the edge of a lake, and dug a hole among the reeds. "Our king has horns!" he whispered into it.

As soon as he had said it, his belly went back to
its normal size and his good spirits returned. He
held up his baggy pants, kicked his heels together,
and went home humming a wordless tune.

Now, it happened that the next day a wandering shepherd came to the same place by the lake with his flock. While the sheep were drinking, he cut himself a reed and made it into a flute. When he put it to his lips and blew, the flute sang out:

"Our king has horns!"

The shepherd was delighted. He led his flock over the mountains and down through the valleys to the singing of the flute.

Eventually he came to the royal city. He played
his flute in the taverns, and every time he blew on
it, the flute sang out:

"Our king has horns!"

It became the talk of the town. The townspeople
were all going around singing, "Our king has horns!"
All, that is, except the young barber, who had
hidden himself in the darkest corner of his house.

When word reached the palace, the king became furious. "Bring me that young barber," he commanded.

The barber was brought before him.

"So you told everyone about my horns!"

"No, Your Majesty," the barber protested. "I didn't tell a single soul!"

"Then why is the whole town singing, 'Our king has horns'?"

"I can't explain it, Your Majesty," said the barber. "Ask the earth if she can speak."

"Insolent nonsense!" roared the king. "You could not keep your word, but I will keep mine. Tomorrow at dawn your head will roll!" And with that he had the barber thrown into prison.

But the young barber was not ready to part with his head. He paced back and forth in his cell for a long time, wondering what to do. Then he lay down on the cold floor and went to sleep.

At dawn the king summoned his whole court to witness the barber's execution. The barber was dragged from prison to the block, and it looked as though nothing could save him. But at the last moment, he held up his hand and called out to the king, "Your Majesty, grant me a final wish, as is the custom in our country."

"What is your final wish?" snapped the king.

"Not long ago a shepherd came to town," said the barber. "They say he has a flute that can sing. I would like to hear this flute before I die."

The king gave orders, and the shepherd was brought in.

"I am told you have a flute that can sing," said the king.

"I have, Your Majesty," said the shepherd.

"There must be some trick to it," said the king. He snatched the flute from the shepherd, examined it carefully, and put it to his lips. The flute sang out:

"Our king has horns!"

The king flew into a rage. He broke the flute over his knee. Then he tore off his crown, threw it down, and stamped on it.

Suddenly realizing what he had done, the king looked up. All his courtiers were staring at him in amazement.

"You see, Your Majesty," said the young barber, "the earth can speak, and reeds can sing, and it's hard to hide the truth, even in the deepest hole or under the highest crown."

The king stood for a long moment without speaking. "Yes, I see," he said at last, glaring sternly at the barber.

The young barber blushed to the roots of his hair.

"Well, well," said the king, "I can hardly punish you for something I myself have revealed to my whole court." And, placing the battered crown back on his head, he proclaimed a general pardon for all the barbers in his realm.

The young barber went home and opened his shop again. If it no longer overflowed with customers as it once had, still he was busy enough for one man. And each month, on the same day, he was summoned to the royal palace, where his skill with the scissors was handsomely rewarded.